# PINGU

## *the Sportsman*

BBC CHiLDReN'S BOOKS

## PINGU GOES ICE SURFING

One day Pingu watched as Mum's washing flapped around in the wind and he had an idea. He rushed off to Dad's work shed.

There he found some pieces of wood to make a
mast. He worked very hard fixing them together.

Now he needed a sail. Mum's sheet would be just the thing. The wind was blowing so hard that it was all Pingu could do to get the sheet off the line.

Then the sheet stuck to him all over so that he looked like a ghost as he made his way back to the work shed.

At last Pingu's ice surfer was ready. The wind
filled the sail and off he went.

It was great fun rushing along at top speed. Pingu zoomed up and down the icy slopes with the wind behind him. He felt as if he was flying.

But suddenly disaster struck. Just as Pingu was
reaching the top of a particularly steep slope, the
wind dropped and both Pingu and the ice surfer
began to slide back down.

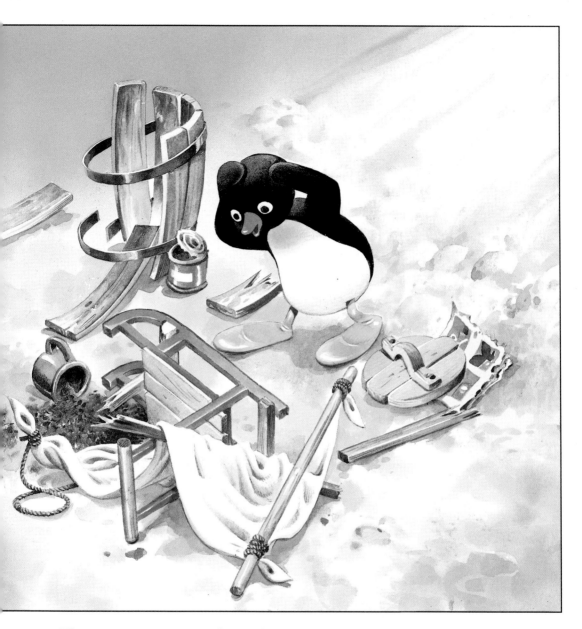

There was a crash at the bottom as the mast snapped. Pingu stared in horror at the wreck of the ice surfer and at Mum's crumpled sheet.

Mum spotted the marks on the sheet straight away and so Pingu had to tell her about the ice surfer.

"Well, there's only one thing for it," said Mum. "You'll have to wash the sheet again yourself."

    Mum gave Pingu some soap and water and he
started to scrub.
    "Has your washing machine broken down?"
asked Robby as he passed by.
    Pingu explained what had happened.

"Well, you won't get the sheet clean like that,"
said Robby. "Let me have a go." Robby set to work,
rubbing the sheet hard with his tail.

Robby washed the sheet so well that when they
put it back on the line it was cleaner than everything
else! Pingu proudly showed the sheet to Mum.

"You've worked hard," said Mum.

"Robby helped me," said Pingu truthfully.

Mum was so pleased with Pingu and Robby that
she gave them each a lovely big fish to eat.
"These are for my washermen," she said and
Pingu and Robby laughed.

## PINGU'S CURLING GAME

There was a loud knock on Pingu's door one afternoon. Pingu went to answer it.

"Sshh," he said to Robby who was outside. "Mum's having a rest."

Robby explained that he was having a game of curling.

I could play with Mum's hot-water bottle, thought Pingu. Very quietly and carefully he took it from her bed and rushed outside.

The hot-water bottle slid well on the ice, but
however hard Pingu tried he couldn't throw it
further than Robby's disc.

"It's not fair. You've been practising," he said to
his friend.

"Watch me throw it," said Robby. "There's nothing to it."

But again, Pingu just couldn't beat Robby.

Pingu was getting cross. "You can't win all the time, Robby," he said.

"Don't make so much noise. I'm trying to read,"
said an old penguin sitting near where the two
friends were playing. "Can't you go and play
somewhere else?"

"What a grumpy old fellow," muttered Pingu.

Pingu had a go at throwing Robby's disc, but then
Robby went and beat him with the hot-water bottle.
Robby roared with laughter. "It's no good, Pingu.
You just haven't got the knack."

Pingu was furious. He picked up the disc and
hurled it with all his strength across the ice. As luck
would have it, it headed straight for the old penguin
and . . .

. . . with a CRASH knocked into his seat and
sent him flying. Pingu and Robby thought this
was a great joke!

"You scamps," roared the old man. "I'll get you
for this." And he began to chase after Pingu. But
every time he got anywhere near, Robby took hold
of his tail and pulled him back.

Pingu retreated quickly through his front door.

Mum was very surprised to see Pingu rush inside.
"What's going on?" she asked as Pingu hid
behind her and the old penguin came marching
after him into the igloo.

Pingu began to explain what had happened and
to say he was sorry, but he was crying so much he
could hardly get his words out. The old penguin
looked sympathetic. "Curling is a difficult sport. I'll
give you a game," he said.

Outside the old penguin threw the disc as hard as he could.

"Well thrown," shouted Robby.

"I used to be good at this game," said the old penguin proudly.

But when it was Pingu's turn he threw his
hot-water bottle even further.

Pingu and Robby were delighted.

"Hurray," they shouted and jumped up and down
in excitement.

## PINGU'S FIRST KISS

One afternoon Pingu met his friends on the ice rink
to practise his skating.

They all skated as gracefully as they could. Pingu
even tried balancing one leg in the air.

"I'm getting bored of this," said one friend. "Why don't we try ice jumps." He showed the other penguins how to skate along the springboard of ice and then take off into the air.

When it came to Pingu's turn he didn't get up
enough speed and he simply toppled off the end of
the springboard.

His friends roared with laughter.

Just then Pingu heard a voice behind him.
"Psst, Pingu, hello." It was Pingi, his new
classmate. She had come to join him on the ice.

Pingu was very pleased to see Pingi.

"I've just been doing ice jumps," he told her
excitedly.

And to show off to Pingi he skated along the springboard and this time took off - WHOOSH - into the air.

"That's wonderful!" shouted Pingi.

Pingi beckoned Pingu over.

"Would you like to come and skate with me on your own?" she asked.

"Oh, yes!" said Pingu, "But I'll have to get away without the others noticing."

So Pingu waited till his friends were busy talking and then skated away as secretly as possible to join Pingi.

Pingu had just reached Pingi when a snowball hit him in the the back.

"You won't escape from us that easily," laughed his friends from behind him.

Pingi and Pingu took no notice. They skated off together making graceful turns and spins on the ice.

"It's much more fun skating together," said Pingu.

When they came to the end of the dance they found themselves alone on the ice and gave each other a big kiss.

Pingu's friends were delighted when Pingi and
Pingu skated by again, swirling round the ice.
"Bravo!" they all clapped and shouted. "Encore!"

Published by BBC Children's Books, an imprint of BBC Worldwide Publishing, Woodlands, 80 Wood Lane, London W12 0TT
First published in Hardback 1991. Illustrations by Tony Wolf. Original text by Sibylle von Flüe.
This edition © BBC Children's Books by arrangement with Dami Editore 1993. Reprinted 1994 (three times). Reprinted 1995.
PINGU © Editoy A G Bertschikon 1991. ISBN 0 563 40335 7
Printed and bound in Great Britain by Cambus Litho, East Kilbride